SNOW JOE

By Carol Greene

Illustrated by Paul Sharp

Children's Press®
A Division of Scholastic Inc.
New York • Toronto • London • Auckland • Sydney
Mexico City • New Delhi • Hong Kong
Danbury, Connecticut

Dear Parents/Educators,

Welcome to Rookie Ready to Learn. Each Rookie Reader in this series includes additional age-appropriate Let's Learn Together activity pages that help your young child to be better prepared when starting school.

Snow Joe offers opportunities for you and your child to talk about the important social/emotional skill of **listening to and engaging others**.

Here are early-learning skills you and your child will encounter in the *Snow Joe* Let's Learn Together pages:

- Communication
- Compare and classify
- Counting

We hope you enjoy sharing this delightful, enhanced reading experience with your early learner.

Library of Congress Cataloging-in-Publication Data

Greene, Carol.
Snow Joe/written by Carol Greene; illustrated by Paul Sharp.

p. cm. — (Rookie ready to learn)

ISBN 978-0-531-25644-2 (library binding) — ISBN 978-0-531-26804-9 (pbk.)

1. Snow—Juvenile literature. I. Sharp, Paul, ill. II. Title. III. Series.

QC926.37.G74 2011 551.57'84—dc22 2011010243

Printed in China. 62

Acknowledgments
© 1982 Paul Sharp, front and back cover illustrations, pages 3–12, 14–26, 28–35, 36–37 snow, Joe, dog, sled, 38–40. Page 34: © Burke/Triolo Producitons/Thinkstock, Comstockimages/Thinkstock, iStockphoto/Thinkstock, Jupiterimages/Thinkstock.

2 3 4 5 6 7 8 9 10 R 18 17 16 15 14 13 12

Joe! Joe!

Snow, Joe!

Snow!

Go, Joe.

Go. Go!

Blow, snow.

Blow at Joe.

Throw, Joe.

Throw that snow.

Roll, Joe.

Roll in snow.

Oh, Joe!

Go, go!

Whoa, Joe!

Whoa . . . oh!

Ho ho!

Ho ho!

Roll, Joe.

Roll that snow.

Grow, snow.

Grow, grow . . .

Oh, Joe!

Show, show!

Slow, Joe.

Go slow.

Slow Joe.

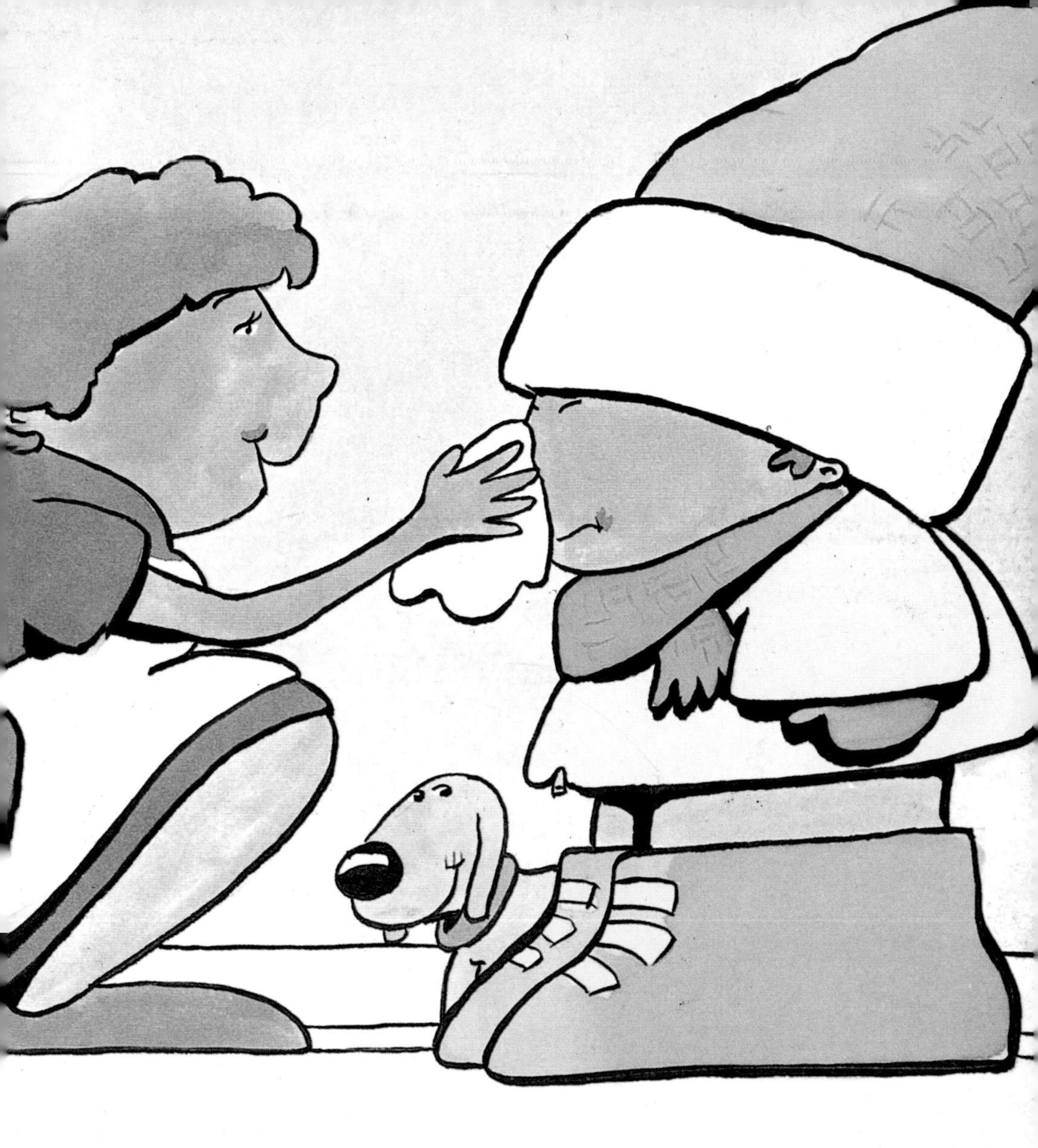

Blow, Joe.

Oh, JOE!

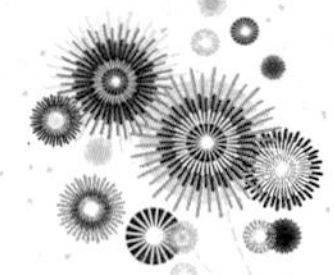

Congratulations!

You just finished reading *Snow Joe* and learned all about having a fun, silly time on a winter day.

About the Author

Carol Greene has written more than 20 books for children, plus stories, poems, songs, and filmstrips. When she isn't writing, she likes to read, travel, sing, do volunteer work at her church—and write some more.

About the Illustrator

Paul Sharp graduated from the Art Institute of Pittsburgh. He works as a freelance artist at his home in Indianapolis, Indiana.

Rookie READY TO LEARN
ACTIVITY BOOK
Snow Joe
Let's learn together!

Winter Fun

Snowflake, snowflake, falling all around,

One by one each snowflake touches ground.

I put on my coat and mittens to play.

Bundled in my hat and scarf, I'm ready for the day.

I build a snowman round and tall.

Then twirling in my ice skates, I have a ball.

I jump on my sled and away I go,

Coasting down the hill and through the snow.

PARENT TIP: Have your child help you "read" the rhyme by naming each object pictured. Later, talk with your child about his favorite things to do in winter. Ask: "What do you like to do when it's cold outside? When it's snowing?"

Rookie READY TO LEARN **VOCABULARY**

Wake Up, Joe!

Joe is in bed when his mom wakes him to play in the snow. Read the poem. Then point to and say who is **in** the bed; who is **beside** the bed; what is **under** the bed; and what hangs **over** the bed.

Joe is **in** bed far from the door.
His dog is **under** the bed, on the floor.
A picture hangs **over** the bed, on one of the walls.
His mother is **beside** the bed. "Get up!" she calls.

PARENT TIP: This activity will help your child build skill in spatial directions and locations, important early math skills, as well as listening and language skills. Afterward, go back to the story. See if your child can find a picture of the dog beside Joe, in front of Joe, behind Joe, and on Joe!

CLASSIFYING

That's So Silly!

Whoa! Look at Joe go! As he sleds, he passes some silly things.

- Look at the picture.
- Point to and name the silly things that you see.

PARENT TIP: Support your child's classifying and critical-thinking skills by sharing this activity. Later, extend the game around the house. Name two items, one that belongs, and one that doesn't belong, in each room. For example, you might say, "There's a stove and an elephant in the kitchen. Which is silly?"

Winter Riddles

Now that you've read the silly story *Snow Joe*, it is your turn to have some fun. Complete these winter rhyming riddles by saying the last word aloud.

People travel on me in the snow.
Down hills they go, go, go!
I can be any color, including red.
Of course, I am a ______!

I fall down quietly day or night.
And cover the world in a blanket of white.
Into a snowman I can roll and grow.
Of course, I am ___________!

PARENT TIP: Help your child build listening and language skills by having her fill in the last word of each riddle. Then go back to page 19 of the story and play a "What Am I Thinking Of?" game. Describe something on the page, without naming it, and see if your child can identify the object by naming and pointing to it in the illustration.

More or Less?

Joe was proud of the snowman he built. Look at the two snowmen. Count the buttons on each snowman. Point to the number on the bottom of the page that shows how many buttons each snowman has.

1 2 3 4 5

Which snowman has more buttons?
Which snowman has fewer buttons?

PARENT TIP: This activity will help build your child's concepts of quantity (more/fewer), skill in counting, and number recognition, all important early math skills. Once your child has counted the buttons on the two snowmen, go back through the book to compare them with the snowman on page 24. Ask your child: "Which snowman has the most buttons?"

Snow Joe Word List (15 Words)

at	ho	roll	that
blow	in	show	throw
go	Joe	slow	whoa
grow	oh	snow	

PARENT TIPS:

For Older Children or Readers:

Ask your child to hunt for the word that starts with *R* on the word list. Then go back to the illustrations of Joe rolling snow on pages 20 and 21 of the story. Have your child find the word *roll* on these pages. Then ask: "What happened to the ball as Joe kept rolling it? What did Joe make with the ball of snow?"

For Younger Children:

Point to the name of the main character, Joe, on the word list. Emphasize the *J* sound as you say the word. Then go back through the story and ask your child to talk about what Joe is doing in each of the illustrations.